Gosling Rescue

Written & Illustrated by
Shirley Montpetit

FriesenPress

<tt>Suite 300 - 990 Fort St
Victoria, BC, V8V 3K2
Canada</tt>

www.friesenpress.com

Copyright © 2020 by Shirley Montpetit
First Edition — 2020

ISBN
978-1-5255-6754-4 (Hardcover)
978-1-5255-6755-1 (Paperback)
978-1-5255-6756-8 (eBook)

1. JUVENILE FICTION, ANIMALS, BIRDS

Distributed to the trade by The Ingram Book Company

Dedicated to
Lena and Patrick

Inspiration
my mom, Mary Burton
who suggested I turn this story into a book

Thank you to
Kevin and Patrick for your patience,
Lena, Mike, Aunt Shirley, and Barb for your input
and
to my publishing team.

CHAPTER 1
The New Nest

*W*et, heavy snow fell serenely, blanketing round **bales of hay** that dotted the field like frosted mini wheats. It was April, and the late spring snow had created a **slough** around one of the **bales**.

A pair of **Canada geese** soared through the sky. Looking over at Father Goose, Mother Goose exclaimed, "Oh dear! We've been looking for a place to nest for a while now! I'm getting rather tired."

Father Goose glanced down. "Yes, this storm does seem to be getting worse. How about there, in that field of **bales**?"

Mother Goose looked relieved. "Yes, one of those will do nicely. The one surrounded with water looks safe." They **descended** quietly down to the **bale** Mother Goose had chosen, a short distance away from the Red Water River. "Ah yes, this will be perfect!" said the joyful mother goose as she began to gather bits of straw to build her nest on top of the **bale**.

Janelle laid down her nature book and stretched. Leaving her nest of blankets on the couch, she gazed out the window at the snow-covered field of **bales**. "Mom, have you seen the binoculars?"

"They're in the library," Mom replied. Her mother was a nature photographer and her dad, a small business owner. They lived, with her younger brother, on an acreage surrounded by Farmer Dick's field on three sides, with the river to the east. Both of Janelle's parents enjoyed the outdoors and had many nature books.

Janelle loved nature too. If she wasn't reading in her free time, she was tramping through the bush or by the river, looking for nests and animal **burrows**. Her long brown hair would become tangled and her socks would fill with burrs. She loved collecting owl pellets at the base of the large dead cottonwood by the river. She would **dissect** the pellets, in the garage, with her mother and put together the bone fragments like a puzzle, to figure out what the owl had eaten. Everything in nature interested Janelle.

Rifling through the library, she grabbed the binoculars to scan the snow-covered field. Her eye caught a small bump on a **bale** not far from the house, near the road that wound around the river. She focused in to see a **Canada goose** sitting on her nest.

She became excited--this meant she would soon be able to watch baby **goslings** hatch!

CHAPTER 2
A Caring Mother

Every day Janelle would hurry to the window, hoping the **goslings** had hatched. Through snow, sleet, rain, and wind, Janelle faithfully watched the goose.

And, through snow, sleet, rain, and wind, the goose faithfully watched over her nest, keeping it safe from coyotes, foxes, and lynx. She only left the nest with her **mate** for one half hour every morning and for one half hour every evening, to feed on left-over field peas from last years' **crop**.

While on her nest, the goose would pick at the **bale** with her teeth to gather more straw. And so the twine that wrapped around the **bale** soon began to **unravel**. Bits of straw drooped down one side. The **bale** looked half ruffled and half smooth.

As the snow melted, Janelle wondered when the eggs would finally hatch. Three weeks had passed since she first spotted the nest. Every day the goose gently nuzzled the eggs with her beak and then **nestled** down, patiently waiting. Janelle, too, would have to be patient.

One evening at suppertime, Farmer Dick's tractor could be heard outside, hauling **bales** across the field. Janelle nervously watched the **bale** that sat by the roadside, badly drooping by now but still topped with the goose nest. The goose and **gander** were away and nowhere to be seen, perhaps on their evening feed.

Janelle held her breath as the tractor approached the road, but then she sighed with relief. The tractor stopped and turned off, just as a van appeared. The van pulled up near the tractor and a woman got out. She handed Farmer Dick a brown paper bag, and he seemed glad to be stopping for his supper. Janelle felt exactly the same way, and so she happily turned to join her parents and brother at the dinner table.

CHAPTER 3

The Terrifying Journey

*W*oah! As the **bale** with the goose nest was lifted, the six unhatched goslings **catapulted** into the air. Suddenly a jerk brought them to rest. More jerks caused the goslings to sway and slosh inside their egg shells as they **lurched** down the field. Drifting through the air, the goslings wondered what was happening.

All of a sudden, the nest bounced as they hit a bump. One of the eggs flipped out of the nest and landed in the field with a smack. Now there were only five.

*Everyone was terrified. The goslings rolled this way and that in their eggs, too scared to peep until they felt themselves dropping downward. With a thump, the **bale** finally came to rest. They heard the sounds of the tractor begin to fade. Then there was quiet.*

*The goslings began to **frantically** peep to each other. "Where are we?" asked one **gosling**. The others didn't know.*

*Soon the sun began to set and the eggs began to cool. The **goslings** wondered where their parents were. Where was their mother's warm body that usually **nestled** down on top of them as evening **approached?***

"I'm cold," peeped one.

"Me too!" peeped another.

"Maybe if we peep loudly, Mother will come," said another hopefully. They all peeped as loudly as they could, but Mother didn't come. Neither did Father.

"I'm going to find Mother!" one gosling declared. The others heard a tapping as the **gosling** began to peck at its thick shell. After a while, a piece of the shell broke off and the gosling tried to stick out its head. But something wasn't right. "I'm so cold . . . and so tired . . . I think I need to sleep now," whispered the gosling softly. And then they heard from the gosling no more.

Now there were only four. They peeped with sadness and fear.

When she finished eating, Janelle took her plate to the sink and glanced out the kitchen window. *Crash!* The dinner plate broke as it slipped from her fingers and dropped into the sink. Everyone jumped and turned to look at Janelle in surprise.

She gasped in terror, her eyes wild. "He took the **bale**! *He took the **bale**!*" Running outside, Janelle saw a **windrow** of **bales** forming at the far end of the field.

He took the bale!

*The **bale** was gone. In its place were two large muddy **ruts** streaking along the ground, and a pair of very **distraught** geese. Honking **frantically,** the mother goose searched the ground, gliding a short distance away. "Oh dear, oh dear! Where are my babies?!" she cried.*

*The gander lifted off and circled overhead, looking for their nest of eggs. "I can't see them anywhere," he called. "In fact, there aren't any **bales** at all!"*

All that remained were a few bits of hay, left broken in the mud.

CHAPTER 4
The Rescue

Janelle slumped on the **veranda** step, breathing the cool spring air. Frogs croaked and crickets hummed in the grass. The **drone** of the farmer's tractor faded.

But her anger had *not* faded. How could this have happened?! Where was the nest now? Had it fallen off the **bale**? Were the eggs on the ground, ruined? Janelle's mind raced.

She had faithfully watched the goose tend to her nest, keeping her eggs warm and determined to hatch her **brood**. Janelle's eyes narrowed. She would not let herself believe that it had all been for nothing.

When Janelle strode back into the house, Mom was cleaning up the broken **shards** of glass. She said firmly to Mom and Dad, "I've got to find the nest." Grabbing her rubber boots and jacket, half tumbling down the back steps, she headed for the field.

The sun was setting and it would soon be dark. There was no tractor. The geese were out of sight.

Janelle ran to where the nest's **bale** had stood. As her eyes adjusted to the dusk, she caught sight of the pair of geese in the distance. Then she looked down at the ground. She saw the **monstrous** tractor tracks through the mud. To the west was the **windrow** of **bales,** a half mile away. If she followed the tracks, she reasoned, she might find the nest.

Encouraged by her plan, she took off toward the **windrow** at a quick run, following the tractor's tracks as best she could. Half way there, she was already out of breath when a flash of something white on the ground caught her eye. She stopped and bent down. It was a broken eggshell. Her eyes blurred with tears as she slipped the shell into her pocket.

She trudged the rest of the way up the field until she finally reached the **windrow** of **bales**.

She scanned the row for the lopsided bale she knew so well by now, and soon she spotted it. She ran to it and gazed upward, holding her breath to listen carefully. Over her pounding heart, she could hear the faint sound of peeping coming from the top of the **bale**. Janelle smiled and took a breath. Had the goslings hatched?

Wildly, Janelle tried to climb the **bale,** but the straw was slippery. She couldn't get a foothold. She quickly scrambled to the other side but still couldn't reach the nest. It was too high. So she decided to dig out the nest.

Burrowing like a **rodent**, Janelle grabbed scratchy clumps of musty straw and threw them to the ground. The nest was large and she had to be careful not to break it. As the peeps became louder, Janelle worked **frantically** to rescue the nest. Finally it was free.

Peep! Peep! Peep!

Carefully taking the peeping nest into her hands, Janelle examined it. She was surprised to see that it was covered with a layer of downy goose feathers. She reached in to stroke the feathers. They felt soft and warm. And Janelle suddenly understood what had confused her for several weeks––how had the eggs stayed warm and hidden from other birds when the mother goose would leave to find food? Why, it was because their mother had left them a cozy blanket! As Janelle peeled the feather blanket back, her eyes widened at the sight of five beautiful wild goose eggs. She was fascinated!

Then her eyes narrowed as she leaned in more closely. One of the eggs looked like it had started hatching. A small **shard** of shell had been **pipped** away, and a tiny bit of wet down could be seen through the crack. Janelle had to move quickly.

With the nest cradled in her arms, she covered the peeping eggs with the down, placed her own jacket over top for extra warmth, and headed for the goslings' home.

The goslings inside their shells were startled by the rustling of straw. They were on the move again, being carried in a gentle rocking motion.

"Now where are we going?" one gosling peeped to the others.

"I don't know. But I'm afraid," said another.

It was slow going in rubber boots and with aching arms. Janelle leaned down toward the nest and whispered, "It's okay. We're just about there."

When she arrived to where the crooked bale had once stood, the goose and gander were nowhere in sight. Janelle carefully put the nest down on the ground, her jacket covering it like a tent. She had to think. What would bring the geese back? She moved back into the field and started peeping as loudly as possible, trying her best to sound like a gosling. It felt silly at first. But she couldn't give up now.

The little goslings heard strange sounds nearby, and were confused. Could that be the sound of another bird? The goslings tried to call back, but they were **exhausted** *by now. Their soft cries could no longer be heard through their shells.*

*Meanwhile, on the Red Water River, Mother and Father Goose **fretted** over their lost family. And then, all of a sudden, they looked up in surprise. Strange calls could be heard in the distance, coming from where their **bale** had been. They lifted off to fly to the spot.*

Glancing toward the sky, Janelle gasped. The parent geese were flying over the trees toward her!

But the geese kept circling overhead and would not land. Janelle began to jump up and down, wave her arms, and make her bird calls even louder. But it was no use. The geese would come no closer.

"Where are our babies?" Mother Goose honked desperately as she looked down at the jumping figure beneath her. "I don't see our babies! Where are they?"

"That strange sound is not our babies," Father Goose said, disappointed. "Come on, Mother. We will keep on searching."

Peep! Peep!

CHAPTER 5

The Plan

As the geese flew off down the field, Janelle lost sight of them. She stomped her foot in frustration. Why hadn't it worked? It was **futile**!

She turned to look down at the nest. Then her hand flew up to her mouth––she suddenly realized what had gone wrong. The geese and gander hadn't flown down because they could not see their nest––it was still covered by Janelle's jacket! She dropped to her knees, yanked the jacket off, and put her ear down to the nest. There was no more peeping coming from the eggs.

Without the mother goose to keep the eggs warm, the goslings might die. Janelle was not going to let that happen. *She* would have to keep them warm.

Scooping up the nest, she carried it into the garage. She knew that heat lamps could be used to warm baby chicks. But she didn't have a heat lamp. She scanned the shelves of the garage urgently. *Oh!* Perhaps a regular desk lamp might work! Fetching the desk lamp from the shelf, she carried the lamp and the nest to a table in the centre of the garage. Gently pushing the remaining feathers on top of the eggs, Janelle set the nest down on the table and turned on the lamp to shine directly over top.

She **yearned** to stay in the garage all night, to hold the eggs in her arms and reassure them it would be alright. But she knew she wouldn't be allowed to. Reluctantly, she left the nest in the garage and went back to her house, to bed.

It was a restless night. Janelle tossed and turned. She thought about the events of the evening. She wondered what the goslings might be doing inside their egg shells. She worried about them. Morning could not come fast enough.

At first light, Janelle raced back to the garage to check on the eggs. Bursting in and heading straight for the table, her heart suddenly felt like it had stopped. Four eggs lay huddled in the warm circle of the desk lamp's light. But the fifth egg seemed to have rolled outside of the light's reach. It perched alone, in a dark shadow in the corner of the nest. Had the little egg made it through the cold night? There was no way to be sure.

Holding her breath, she tilted her ear as close as she could get to the eggs. Then her lips began to stretch slowly into a grin of joy. The sound of faint peeping reached her ears. They had survived! Relieved, Janelle had to see if their parents had returned.

Quiet as a mouse, she peered out the garage door. There, in the field, were the goose and gander. Cradling the nest in her arms, Janelle carried it across the lawn and placed it down on the spot that had once held the droopy **bale**. Then she scurried back to her house and peered out the window.

The pair moved toward the nest.

*Mother Goose let out a honk of disbelief. "Could this be our babies in their nest?" She lowered her head to the eggs and then shifted to **nestle** down into the nest. "Oh, my beautiful babies! I thought I'd never see you again," whispered the mother goose. Father Goose stood proudly nearby, his chest puffed up like a balloon ready to explode. At last they were reunited with their unborn babies.*

CHAPTER 6
The New Family

For three more days Janelle watched the geese through her binoculars. On the fourth day, a **wisp** of yellow could be seen. From her living room window, she watched in amazement as tiny yellow balls of fluff scurried about in the field. The gander looked on lovingly, protective of his family.

In less than an hour, the pair led a line of healthy goslings through the rough, stubbly field and toward the river.

Tossing her binoculars aside, Janelle scrambled into her boots and jacket, and ran out onto the **veranda**. Excitedly, she scanned the field to catch a glimpse of the geese before they disappeared from view. Spotting their tiny, waddling figures up ahead, she began to quietly follow behind them at a safe distance. To get to the river, they would have to journey a half a mile and then cross the road.

As she passed by the deserted nest that had been left behind by the new family, her eyes were drawn to something she had not expected to see: Two eggs still remained in the nest, unhatched. She bent down to take a closer look, and then tears filled her eyes. She recognized the first unhatched egg immediately--it was the one that had already been cracked and partially opened when she fetched the nest from the windrow.

Beside it lay a second unhatched egg--probably the one that had rolled into the cold darkness of the garage, Janelle reasoned. Sadly, she reached out and touched the eggs tenderly. Then she reached into her pocket and withdrew the pieces of the smashed egg shell that she had found on the ground on that adventurous evening, four days ago. She placed them gently beside the other two eggs in the nest, covered them up with down, and then stood up to go.

She hadn't been able to save these three eggs. But she could still make sure that the new family made it to the river safely.

Janelle **composed** herself and carried on down the field, catching up with the new family. As she watched the goslings run beside their parents--stumble, fall, recover, stumble, fall, and recover--she was amazed at how **determined** and strong they were. The goslings had to sprint the length of the field as their parents walked at a steady pace toward the river. It seemed to take forever.

"Hey! Wait for me!" peeped one.
"I need a rest!" cried another.

As they finally reached the road, the five geese cautiously crossed to the other side. The gander led his **brood** down the steep grass-covered bank to the river's edge. After a brief rest, they entered the river, the goslings floating close at their parents' side.

"It's so cold and wet!" peeped one of the goslings.

"Stick together by me, little ones, and you'll stay warm," Mother Goose reassured them.

Janelle watched them swim away. Then she turned to head back home.

Slowly making her way back across the field, Janelle smiled as she thought of the goslings. For five weeks, she had lovingly watched over their little eggs. She had done everything she could to rescue them when they were in trouble. And now they were safe, happily swimming behind their mother and father on the banks of the Red Water River, as they should be.

Perhaps the goslings would never know that a little girl had cared enough to save their lives. But Janelle would always know. And Janelle would always go on caring. And that is enough to save the world.

The End

GLOSSARY

Attempt: To try

Bale: A large, wrapped bundle of hay

Brood: A group of young birds born to the same mother

Burrows: Holes or tunnels dug by animals for a hiding place or home

Canada goose: A common North American goose with a black head and neck, a white chinstrap, and a loud, trumpeting call

Catapult: To spring up and forward with force

Compose: To make yourself calm or ready

Crop: A plant that is grown in a large batch

Descend: To move downward to a lower position

Dissect: To cut something open to examine it

Distraught: To feel worried and afraid

Drone: To make a low, steady hum

Exhausted: To make tired; wear out

Frantic: Very excited by worry or fear

Fret: To feel worried or uneasy

Futile: Useless

Gander: A male goose

Gosling: A very young goose

Lurch: A sudden movement

Mate: The partner of a bird, other animal, or person

Monstrous: Large and so ugly it is scary

Nestle: To get comfortable; to settle on, within, or against something

Perch: A place where something sits

Pip: A crack or chip in the shell of an egg, which happens when the chick/gosling begins to hatch

Rifling: To search through

Rodent: A group of nibbling animals, such as rats, mice, squirrels, hamsters, porcupines, and others

Rut: A long, deep track made by tires

Shard: A piece of a broken object; a fragment of eggshell

Slough: A swampy or marsh-like hollow or place

Unravel: To undo something

Veranda: A large, open porch attached to a house

Vicious: To show angry feelings

Windrow: A row of hay bales, before they are stacked

Wisp: A small bit

Yearn: To have a strong wish for something

Lightning Source UK Ltd.
Milton Keynes UK
UKHW050900161120
373349UK00008B/174

9 781525 567544